Fox
in a
Box

EVA KLASSEN

illustrated by
Leanne Thiessen

BIG MIND
BOOKS

FOX IN A BOX

Text copyright © 2019 by Eva Klassen and Big Mind Books
Illustrations copyright © 2019 by Leanne Thiessen and Big Mind Books

For wholesale information, please email hello@bigmind.ca

Designed by Ninth and May Design Co.
Printed in Canada by Friesens Corporation

FIRST EDITION

ISBN: 978-1-9992448-0-4 hardcover
ISBN: 978-1-9992448-1-1 paperback
ISBN: 978-1-9992448-2-8 ebook

BIG MIND
BOOKS.ca

Printed on 100% PCW Recycled Paper

In the deep dark woods
down a long winding road,
lives a sly little creature
with a long fuzzy nose.

Black as night,
square as can be,
perched on a shelf
and bulging at
the seams…

is
his
box.

Fox loves his box.

Fox loves
everything IN
his box.

He loves
his socks!

Knitted and cozy
with spicks and spocks.
For every occasion,
especially long walks.

Fox loves
his rocks.

Smooth and flat,
sharp and round,
in every colour
that's ever been found!

Fox loves
his blocks.

For stacking and building
and blowing and knocking.
And the moment before
the tower starts rocking!

And don't forget
his clocks.

With faces and hands,
the clicks, the clocks,
all with different
ticks and tocks.

But before Fox knew it,
a pile of things
grew into a
mountain of stuff,

and getting into his box
was getting quite tough!

Then Fox had it,
a brilliant idea!

He'd give some of his things to his best friend Sofia!

Perhaps a clock,
Fox knew she had none.